Jenny Goes to Sea

MORE BOOKS ABOUT JENNY
BY ESTHER AVERILL

Jenny and the Cat Club:
A Collection of Favorite Stories about Jenny Linsky

Jenny's Birthday Book

Jenny's Moonlight Adventure

Hotel Cat

JENNY GOES TO SEA

Story and Pictures by
Esther Averill

THE NEW YORK REVIEW CHILDREN'S COLLECTION
New York

THIS IS A NEW YORK REVIEW BOOK
PUBLISHED BY THE NEW YORK REVIEW OF BOOKS

Published in the United States of America by
The New York Review of Books, 1755 Broadway,
New York, NY 10019
www.nyrb.com

Library of Congress Cataloging-in-Publication Data

Averill, Esther Holden.
Jenny goes to sea / by Esther Averill.
p. cm. — (New York Review children's collection)
Summary: The little black cat named Jenny, along with her brothers and their
owner Captain Tinker, sails around the world on a ship called the
Sea Queen.
ISBN 1-59017-155-1 (alk. paper)
[1. Cats—Fiction. 2. Ocean travel—Fiction. 3. Ships—Fiction.]
I. Title. II. Series.
PZ7.A935Jeg 2005
[Fic]—dc22
                                2004029981

Cover design by Louise Fili Ltd.

This book is printed on acid-free paper.
Manufactured in China by P. Chan & Edward, Inc.
1 3 5 7 9 10 8 6 4 2

Distributed to the trade by Publishers Group West

FOR

KRP

FROM THE SHIP'S CAT & THE CAT CLUB

Contents

Ready for the Sea 7

The Ship's Cat 20

South Africa 32

Zanzibar 44

Fortunes Told in the Old Bazaar 53

On Their Way to the East 63

All Ashore in Singapore 69

Storm in the Gulf of Siam 79

Checkers Slips Away 83

Jenny Holds the Ship 96

Hammocks for All 105

Edward Writes a Poem 111

Home from the Sea 118

A map of the *Sea Queen's*
voyage around the world 30-31

Ready for the Sea

This was their last night at home—their last few hours on land. In the morning these three young cats would get on board a ship and go to sea.

Edward, the oldest in the family, looked through the open window of the living-room.

"The moon is high. It's time to say good-by," he said. "Jenny, you go first."

The little black cat, Jenny Linsky, leaped
to the window sill and down upon the
garden. Her brother, Checkers, who was
black and white and somewhat older than

8

herself, went next. Edward, the brownish tiger cat, brought up the rear.

For a moment the three cats stood together, gazing at the maple tree that grew in the far corner of the garden.

Then Jenny said, "I guess all the Cat Club is there by now. Dear me, I hate to say good-by."

"But we'll have fun at sea," said Checkers, rubbing his cheek lovingly against hers. "Besides, Jenny, you were the one who helped arrange the trip with Captain Tinker. Don't you remember?"

Jenny did remember. She remembered the day when she had first felt that their dear master, Captain Tinker, might be going somewhere on a journey. She had jumped up on his knees and kissed his face and begged him in a dozen different ways to take his three cats with him. The Captain had finally agreed.

"And we'll come back here someday," Checkers was saying. "I know we will because Captain Tinker has left my red retrieving ball and all our other toys right where they belong."

"Just the same, it's hard to say good-by," said Jenny.

But as she and her brothers moved toward the Club meeting ground beneath the maple tree, her heart began to beat excitedly. All the members of the Club were sitting in a circle with Mr. President at the head. And on Mr. President's right—just imagine— sat the fire cat, Pickles, who worked for the New York City Fire Department.

"Pickles must have got the night off to say good-by to us," thought Jenny to herself. "My! What an honor."

As she squeezed herself into the circle between her brothers, Mr. President said, "The meeting will please come to order."

Everyone sat very straight.

"This is a special meeting," continued Mr. President. "It has been called so that the Cat Club may bid farewell to three of our junior members who are going off to sea. Their names are—"

"Jenny! Checkers! Edward!" cried the Cat Club.

"They're going off to sea with their good master, Captain Tinker," said Mr. President. "And since the Captain kindly lets the Cat Club use his garden, we shall here and now wish him a happy voyage."

The members turned their faces toward Captain Tinker's pink brick house. He happened to be standing at the open window.

"Happy voyage! And a safe return!" they cried.

The old sea captain raised his hand, as if to thank them. Then he disappeared.

"As for the voyage itself," said Mr. President, "we've had difficulty getting facts. Voyages at sea are hard for land cats like ourselves to understand, except when other cats explain things. Of course, we felt it in our bones that Captain Tinker might be planning a long trip."

"Ah! felt it in our bones," the Cat Club murmured.

"But it is not enough to feel things in one's bones," Mr. President said briskly. "Our Cat Club wishes facts whenever possible. Tonight I have some facts for you. Will Sinbad and The Duke report?"

Sinbad and The Duke, those two raggedy cats who ran wherever they pleased on the city streets, were sitting side by side. And

now they spoke together, helping one another out.

"We managed to get to the waterfront," they said. "That's where the ships come in from the sea. Along the waterfront we met a longshore cat—a working cat—named Bill. Bill told us Captain Tinker's luggage has been put on board the good ship *Sea Queen. And the* Sea Queen's *going to sail around the world.*"

"Around the world," thought Jenny to herself. "I wonder what that means. It sounds very far."

But there was no time in which to wonder. At a signal from Mr. President, the Club burst into a song in honor of Jenny and her brothers. The music was the old Club marching tune, but the words were new and beautiful. Jenny suspected that Edward, who loved poetry, might have written them. She glanced at him out of the corner of her eye. He was sitting very still, trying to look innocent. But when the Club repeated the song, his tail swayed happily to the lilt of the words.

"Heigh ho!
And away they go!
Three young cats to sea.

Far will they roam,
But may they come home
To us
Safe from the sea.

Oh!
Safe from the sea."

Still singing the song, the Club accompanied Jenny and her brothers to their home.

"I wish all of you were coming, too!" cried Jenny.

"Some of us must stay on land to carry on the business of the Cat Club," observed Mr. President.

Then, at a wave of his paw, the meeting broke up, and the members of the Club drifted slowly across the garden toward their homes. Some lived in houses by the garden. Others, like the fire cat, Pickles, had to climb over the tall board fence and go to other streets.

Checkers and Edward went inside their house to make sure their traveling baskets were in good order. But the little black cat, Jenny Linsky, remained on the window sill to take a last look at the garden she loved so dearly.

Presently she heard someone climbing over the top of the board fence. It was the big, spotted fire cat, Pickles, who came running toward her. When he reached her house, he touched the brim of his fire helmet with a most respectful paw.

"Jenny," he said, "you may be gone a long, long time."

"Yes, Pickles," she said shyly.

"You'll see many far-off lands," continued Pickles. "Maybe you'll meet famous cats. Please don't forget your old friend, Pickles."

"Pickles! How could I ever forget you?" exclaimed Jenny. "Think of all the good

times—and the hard times—we've had together. Oh, I almost wish I didn't have to go to sea."

"Nonsense," cried Pickles gaily. "It isn't every cat who gets a chance to see the wonders of the world."

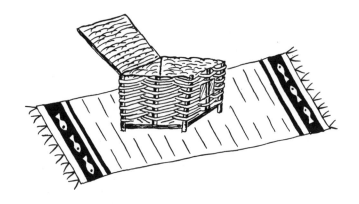

The Ship's Cat

Next morning Jenny, Checkers and Edward were put into their traveling baskets and taken by their master in a taxi to the ship. The three cats were safe in their room, or cabin, as the *Sea Queen* slowly left her dock. Soon the engines of the ship began to throb, and she gained speed. After a while a wind blew past the small, round window of the cabin, the waves grew higher, and the ship rolled on the open sea.

The cats were kept in their cabin until the following morning. By then they were used to the roll of the *Sea Queen*. After a breakfast of their favorite canned food, they felt like exploring the ship. Their master, Captain Tinker, tied Jenny's red wool scarf around her neck. It was the scarf she wore whenever she went out.

"Now you're ready," he said.

He picked her up in his arms and carried her, along with her brothers, to a flight of stairs.

"Follow your noses down the stairs," said the Captain. "You'll meet someone who will help you. I'll wait here until you find him."

They walked carefully down the stairs, sniffing the air as they went.

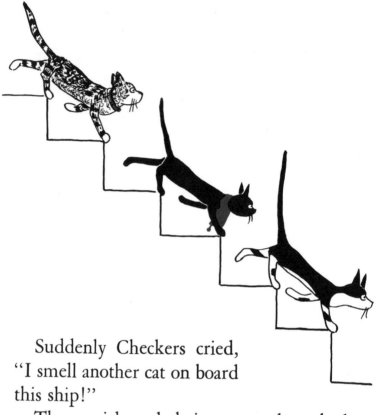

Suddenly Checkers cried,
"I smell another cat on board
this ship!"

They quickened their pace and reached
a sunny deck. Above the deck swung a cat-
size hammock. In the hammock lay a cat,
with a white hind leg dangling lazily over
the edge.

22

Edward was the first to speak. "Please, sir, is this the good ship *Sea Queen*?"

"Aye, that it is," replied a salty voice. "And for your further information, what you see out there is the Atlantic Ocean."

They gazed beyond the rails of the ship and saw the green waters of the Atlantic.

"We're Captain Tinker's cats," continued Edward.

"I've met your master," said the voice in the hammock. "He brought me down a whiff of catnip. He's a gentleman, indeed."

With those words, the cat jumped from his hammock, landed neatly on deck and faced the three young travelers.

They stared at him, wondering who he was.

He seemed older than Edward, and yet
not old at all. His eyes were as green as the
ocean; his fur as white as the foam on the
waves. On the top of his head, between his
ears, grew a patch of gray fur, like a woolen
cap that would protect him in rough
weather.

"I'm the ship's cat," he explained. "My
name is Tar. Jack Tar. Your master has
asked me to take charge of you. And so it
might be wise for me to learn your names."

"Mr. Tar," said Edward, "this is my sister, Jenny. This is my brother, Checkers.
I am Edward."

24

"You don't look anything alike," the ship's cat observed pleasantly.

Checkers said, "I can explain things. I met Edward when he and I were roaming the streets of New York, looking for a home. We promised to be brothers. Then Jenny found us. She was Captain Tinker's cat. She asked her master to adopt us, and he did. So now we're all in the same family."

"That really does explain things," said Jack Tar. "But I wasn't trying to pry into family affairs. It's just that, traveling around the world the way I do, I've grown interested in all different kinds of things. Cats, for example."

"Good cats and bad cats?" asked Checkers.

"No, that isn't what I mean," replied Jack Tar. "I mean the different races, or breeds, or families of cats you'll find in the old, far-off countries of the world. As you know, American cats like ourselves all came from somewhere, at least our ancestors did. For example, I'd say that Jenny and Edward and I have come down from the noble cats of ancient Egypt."

"Goodness," Jenny thought to herself. She had never even heard of Egypt.

"And me?" asked Checkers anxiously. "Where did I come from?"

Jack Tar answered, "Some of your ancestors came from Egypt, too. But one of them, maybe your grandfather, came from another wonderful land—the country of Siam."

"How can you tell?" asked Checkers.

Jack Tar said, "There are certain things about you that remind me of the cats who live in Siam. That pointed face of yours, and the fur that grows like a hood around your eyes, and your long thin tail that looks like a whip. These things would tell me, if nothing else did.

"Of course," continued Mr. Tar, "if you were entirely Siamese, your colors would be different. You'd be cream and chocolatey, instead of black and white."

Jenny looked steadily at the ship's cat.

27

"Mr. Tar, I think black and white is very beautiful," she said loyally.

"And so it is," agreed Jack Tar.

Then he turned to Checkers, saying, "The cats of Siam have reason to be proud. In olden times, they lived in the Royal Palace and ranked higher than the king."

"Where is Siam?" asked Checkers.

"In the East of the world," replied Jack Tar, waving a paw toward the distant horizon.

"Have you been in Siam?" asked Checkers.

Jack Tar nodded.

"What's it like?" continued Checkers. His eyes by now were shining like two little moons.

"Strange and wonderful, like many countries in the East," replied Jack Tar. "Our ship calls at Siam. You'll have a chance to see things for yourself."

"So we're going to Siam!" cried Checkers joyfully. "How soon will we get there?"

"Young cat, you can't hurry things at sea," said Jack Tar. "Before we reach Siam, we must cross the Atlantic Ocean and the Indian Ocean and the Gulf of Siam and make three stops along the way."

The ship's cat looked thoughtfully at the three young travelers and added, "You and I will be together many months on board this ship. To make things easy, please don't call me mister. Call me Jack."

Jenny thought to herself, "Jack is such a lovely name. Pickles is a good name, too."

Memories of her old friend, Pickles, flashed through her mind. But land seemed far away. Here, wherever she looked, she saw only the green waves of the Atlantic Ocean.

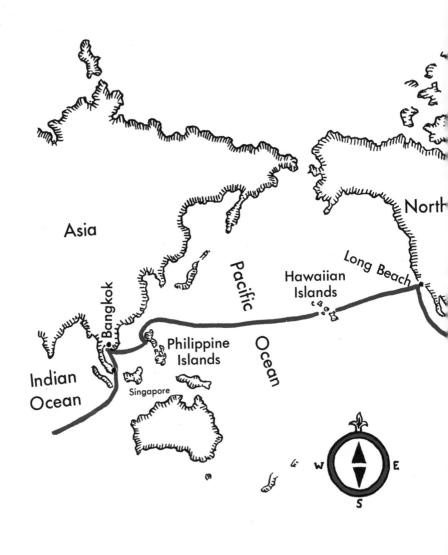

Route of the good ship *Sea Queen*
on her voyage around the world

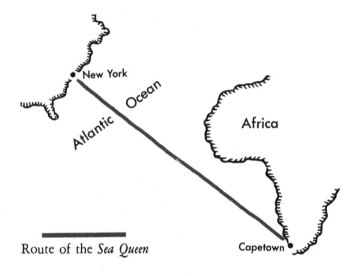

Route of the *Sea Queen*

South Africa

Jenny, as well as her brothers, quickly made friends with Jack.

One day she asked him, "How long have you sailed in the *Sea Queen*?"

"Ever since I was a kitten," he replied.

"What made you think of going to sea?" asked Edward, who had been listening.

32

"I lost my home in New York," said Jack. "So I climbed on board the *Sea Queen*. I'd heard she needed a ratcatcher."

Then Jack went on to say, "Most ships take along a cat to keep the rats away. If we gave those horrid creatures a chance, they'd eat our food and chew our freight."

"Freight?" queried Checkers. "What's freight?"

"I thought you knew," said Jack.

"We're only land cats," Checkers said rather humbly. "We don't know much about ships and the sea."

"That's true," Jack agreed. "And it's up to me to explain things like freight. Freight is goods. It's the stuff we're paid to carry from country to country. Things like the new American cars we're taking to lands that need them. We also carry a few passengers—people who pay their way. But freight's the most important thing we handle."

Jenny asked anxiously, "Is our master, Captain Tinker, just a passenger?"

"Goodness!" exclaimed Jack. "Your master is managing our freight on this trip. He's what we call Master of Freight."

"Master of Freight!" Jenny thought to herself. "I might have known that Captain Tinker was helping the *Sea Queen*."

Jenny suddenly felt she belonged with the ship.

"The *Sea Queen* seems like home," she told Jack.

"She's home to me," he admitted, pressing his paw affectionately against the deck.

From that time onward, Jenny, Checkers and Edward enjoyed every moment of their life on board this floating home. Most of their waking hours were spent with Jack. They strolled the sunny decks with him and climbed the ropes and tried to count the whitecaps on the ocean waves. Overhead the sky was blue as blue could be, for

the *Sea Queen* was following the Fair
Weather route across the South Atlantic.

Four weeks went by. Jenny almost didn't care if she saw land again. But slowly and surely the *Sea Queen* was drawing near South Africa.

One bright morning Jack called down from the bridge on top of the ship, "Land ahead!"

Jenny, Checkers and Edward dashed to the rail. On the horizon they could see a blur. The blur grew bigger and more distinct. And they felt the thrill that grips an ocean traveler when he sights land.

After a while the *Sea Queen* entered the harbor of Capetown. Around the harbor sprawled a city with a huge mountain right at her back.

The three cats stared at the mountain.

Its top was flat like a table. On this table lay a cloud as white as the fairest cloth.

"That mountain is called Table Mountain," said Jack when he came down from the bridge. "It's one of the wonders of the world."

"What lies behind the mountain?" asked Checkers.

"Great jungles and plains, filled with lions and tigers," answered Jack. "I've never been that far. But I've been told that those lions and tigers are hundreds of times bigger than cats like ourselves."

"Wow!" exclaimed Checkers. "I'm glad we don't have to leave this ship."

"You're safe. Don't worry," said Jack quickly. "As for myself, I'm going ashore on special business."

By now, the *Sea Queen* had been tied to the dock. And from her deck to the dock stretched the gangplank down which one could walk ashore. Jenny moved over with her brothers and Jack and sat near the gangplank. They watched the passengers go down it with their cameras. After the passengers walked some of the sailors.

"It's my turn now," said Jack.

"Take care of yourself," cried Jenny. "That gangplank looks steep and dangerous."

But Jack stepped nimbly down it and disappeared among the buildings of the city.

Suddenly life seemed dull aboard the *Sea Queen*.

"What shall we do?" asked Checkers.

"Let's visit Captain Tinker," Jenny suggested.

"Yes," agreed Edward. "We might learn about the shipping business."

They found the Master of Freight on the deck where the derricks stood. These derricks had long steel arms that were busily taking American cars from the hold of the ship and swinging them to the docks.

After a number of cars had been un-
loaded, men carried aboard large bags, or
bales, of wool that had been clipped from
African sheep. A piece of white wool
drifted from the top of a bag and fell on

the deck. Jenny touched the wool with her paw. It was as soft as the little red scarf her master had knitted for her.

"This is very educational," Edward observed.

But Checkers said what was really on their minds: "I wonder what Jack Tar is up to."

"I hope he doesn't miss the boat," Jenny said anxiously.

The very thought that the *Sea Queen* might have to sail without Jack made them shudder. So they said good-by to their master and moved over to the top of the gangplank, where they waited patiently for Jack.

Lunchtime came. Still there was no sign of him or of any of the sailors and passengers who had gone ashore. But the three cats did not go down to the kitchen, where the cook let them eat with Jack. Instead, they waited at the top of the gangplank for their friend to return.

Hours went by. Then, toward late afternoon, the sailors came back to the ship. After them straggled the passengers, some of them merrily singing.

"They must have had a high old time," observed Checkers.

"But where is Jack?" asked Jenny.

All at once a white cat streaked across the dock and dashed up the gangplank. Two minutes later the *Sea Queen* gave three long whistles and the gangplank was pulled up.

"Jack, what a scare you gave us," said Jenny. "We thought you'd miss the ship."

"Not I," declared Jack.

He brushed a paw across his face to clean his whiskers. But on them lingered a fishy smell.

"Jack Tar," said Edward, "you've been eating something special."

"Special business?" asked Checkers brightly.

"South African lobster tails," honest Jack admitted. "They're a famous dish in this part of the world."

LOBSTER

Edward's mouth began to water. "It must be very educational to go ashore and taste the special dishes in the different ports," he hinted.

Jack thought a moment. Then he turned to Jenny and asked her, "Would it frighten you to go ashore?"

Jenny remembered how steep the gangplank had looked as it dangled from the ship to the dock. But she said, "I'll manage."

So it was agreed that at the next port of call Jenny, Checkers and Edward would go ashore with the ship's cat.

43

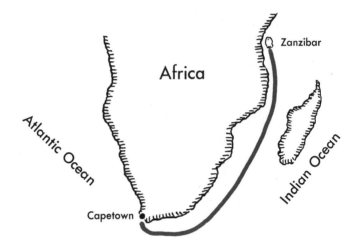

Zanzibar

"Zanzibar will be our next stop," announced Jack.

The strange-sounding word Zanzibar made Jenny and her brothers tingle with delight. Edward declared it was the loveliest word he had ever heard. He rolled it softly on his tongue: *Zanzibar! Zanzibar! Zanzibar!*

44

To reach Zanzibar, the *Sea Queen* had to sail around the southern tip of Africa and cross the foaming boundary where the waters of the Atlantic and the Indian Oceans meet. Then she pursued her course northeastward across the Indian Ocean.

Presently the ship fell in with a wind.

Jack said, "We'll have this wind at our back all the way to Zanzibar. It's called the monsoon."

He explained that the monsoon blew up from the southeast during six months of the year, just as it was blowing now.

"Then the monsoon turns around," he said. "During the next six months it blows down from the northwest."

"The monsoon isn't like the winds at home," Checkers observed. "Our winds blow every which way."

"We're far from home," commented Jack. "This is the Indian Ocean, where everything is different."

After many days at sea, they passed a small vessel with a single jaunty sail set crosswise on her mast.

"That kind of ship is called a dhow," explained Jack. "It's the oldest type of freighter in the world. Dhows let the monsoon blow them to their ports of call."

They passed a second dhow, and a third.

"We're getting close to Zanzibar," said Jack.

A blur on the horizon grew clearer and bigger, and they saw the island of Zanzibar,

lying like a green jewel in the bright blue
sea. On the shore of the island stretched the
low, white town of Zanzibar.

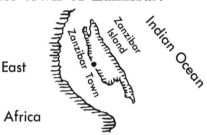

They entered the harbor of the town
and dropped anchor.

"The water isn't deep enough for us to
go all the way to the town," Jack explained.
"That little boat you see coming toward us
will carry us to the dock. She's called a
lighter."

The lighter drew up alongside the *Sea
Queen*, and a gangplank was lowered to the
lighter's deck. The regular passengers
walked down the gangplank first, and then
the sailors. When the cats' turn came, Jack
led the way. Jenny followed him, with

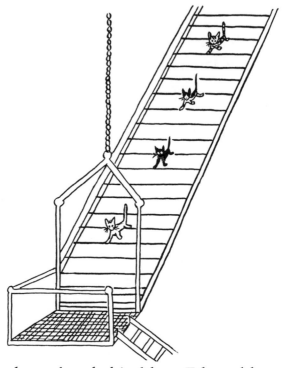

Checkers close behind her. Edward brought up the rear. Although Jenny had three boy cats to protect her, the gangplank made her dizzy. Still she managed to get down it safely.

"Good work," Jack told her when she reached the lighter.

Then the lighter chugged to the dock. Here another gangplank was lowered, and again Jack led the way. Before she knew it, Jenny found herself standing on the dock.

"Land," she murmured, "land."

It seemed strange not to have the *Sea Queen* rolling beneath her paws. But Checkers had already got his land legs.

"Jack," he said eagerly, "where do we go from here?"

"I'll take you to a big hotel for lunch," Jack answered. "Afterward we'll visit the bazaar, where all the shops are. In the bazaar lives an Abyssinian cat who tells fortunes."

An Abyssinian cat who tells fortunes! A meal in a big hotel! Jenny had never eaten in a hotel—not even in New York. And this was Zanzibar. How glad she was that she had worn her scarf. She wished to look her best as she accompanied the ship's cat and her brothers through the sunny town.

It seemed like a town right out of a fairy tale. On the streets walked Arab men in long white robes, with fezzes, red or white, on their heads. And in the air hung a heavy perfume—a delicious, spicy scent.

"That's cloves you smell," said Jack. "They're buds from clove trees. The Arabs dry the buds and ship them all over the world. People like cloves in their food—I don't know why."

Branch of clove buds

Edward asked cautiously, "What do we eat when we reach the hotel?"

"I recommend the oysters," replied Jack. "Oysters from the Indian Ocean are a favorite food in Zanzibar."

"Oysters for me," Edward agreed.

"And me," Jenny said.

"Me, too," said Checkers.

Soon they reached the hotel kitchen. Jack was the first one through the doorway.

"Jack! Jack Tar!" a man cried happily.

Then the man caught sight of Jenny, Checkers and Edward and let forth a flow of words in a strange language. From the tone of his voice one could tell he was expressing his surprise at seeing the three young travelers.

"That's the cook himself," Jack told them. "He speaks Arabic, but I can make him understand us."

Jack rubbed his back affectionately against the cook's ankles.

"Jackie! Jackie Tar!" said the cook, leaning down to stroke Jack's head.

The cook asked Jack a question in Arabic.

Jack answered by walking to a table where one of the cook's helpers was opening the shells of oysters. Jack stood on his hind legs and touched the edge of the table with a front paw.

The cook understood, and the four cats were soon eating oysters from gay plates on the floor.

"Jack, those oysters were delicious," Edward declared, after he had licked his plate clean.

"Let's thank the cook and say good-by," said Jack.

Edward asked, "Is it polite to eat and run?"

"The cook will understand," Jack answered. "He knows that tourists like yourselves—folks who travel just for fun— must visit the bazaar."

Jack and the young tourists walked over to the cook. By way of thanks they looked at him with grateful eyes. The cook gave each of the cats a gentle pat. And that is how they said good-by.

The cats returned to the street.

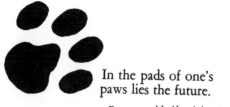

In the pads of one's paws lies the future.

From an old Abyssinian proverb

Fortunes Told in the Old Bazaar

"Now I'll take you to the bazaar—the place with all the little shops," said Jack. "You'll meet the Abyssinian cat who tells fortunes."

"What's an Abyssinian cat?" asked Checkers.

"Abyssinians are members of the oldest race, or family, of cats in the world," replied Jack. "The Abyssinian in the bazaar can trace her family back to thousands of years ago."

"Does she speak Abyssinian?" Edward inquired.

Jack laughed.

"She speaks good old cat talk, just like you and me," he said. "As a matter of fact, cats all over the world speak the same language. In this respect, we're smarter than humans."

"What is the Abyssinian's name?" asked Jenny.

"Her real name is very long," answered Jack. "For fun, I call her Abbie."

They walked through narrow, winding streets lined with white or colored houses that had huge, mysterious doors of dark, carved wood studded with brass nailheads.

After a while the cats reached the bazaar, where some of the tourists from the *Sea Queen* were buying rugs and other souvenirs.

Jack hurried his party into a shop that sold brass cowbells. In a room in the back

of the shop, on a table, sat a cat whose fur was the lovely reddish gray that belongs to the Abyssinian family. She was washing her face in a mirror, with her back to the door. In the mirror she must have caught the reflection of Jack and his three friends, for she called out, "Jackie! Jackie, my boy!"

"Greetings, Abbie," said Jack. "How have you been since we last met?"

"Quite well, Jackie," she replied, as she continued to wash in the mirror.

"It's an American mirror," she explained. "It came on the last voyage of the *Sea Queen*. There, now. I've finished my toilet."

The Abyssinian turned around slowly, and one could see that, old though she was, her face had kept its royal beauty. One might wonder what strange fate had brought her to the bazaar in Zanzibar.

She looked carefully at Jenny and her brothers, but addressed her words to Jack.

"Tourists?" she queried.

He nodded.

"From the States?" she asked.

"Yes, they're from New York," answered Jack. "They've come along to see the world. Abbie, as a special favor, would you tell their fortunes?"

The Abyssinian half closed her eyes and hunched her shoulders as if she were throwing around them a cloak that would separate her from the others in the room.

"I'll take the little black one first," she said finally. "Jump up here, my dear."

Jenny hesitated. She had never heard her fortune told. What if she should learn that something terrible might happen to her to-morrow or in the days to come? But she mustn't let the others know she was fright-ened. She took a deep breath and jumped up on the table.

"Hold out your right front paw," said the Abyssinian. "I'll read what I see in it."

Jenny held out a steady paw. The Abys-sinian gazed at it.

"A small paw, but a brave paw," she announced. "You'll do something brave before the *Sea Queen* ends her voyage."

Jenny wondered to herself, "Me do something brave? Why, I'm even afraid of the gangplank."

"I'll take the tiger cat next," said the Abyssinian.

Jenny jumped to the floor, and Edward took her place on the table.

The Abyssinian glanced at his paw and

then at his well-filled stomach.

"You like good food," she observed.

Edward, who hated to be teased about his love of food, protested. "I like other things, too, especially the sound of pretty words."

"Yes," agreed the Abyssinian. "I can see in your paw that you enjoy words. Before the voyage is over, you will write something beautiful."

"A poem," sighed Edward. "I should love to write a poem."

"That's what I was about to say," remarked the Abyssinian. "You'll write the best poem you have ever written."

Edward jumped to the floor, and Checkers leaped to the table. The Abyssinian glanced at his long, Siamese-like tail and at the curious patterns that marked his fur. Then she studied the pink pads of his paw.

"A difficult paw to read," she declared. "It may be that you'll do something naughty."

Checkers looked puzzled.

"Where?" he asked. "Where will I be naughty?"

The Abyssinian closed her eyes and murmured, "In the East of the world."

Then she said briskly, "Come, Jack Tar, let me read your paw. You know I always read it when you come to Zanzibar."

But Jack had moved to the doorway.

"Thank you, Abbie," he said. "On my next trip to Zanzibar, I'll have my fortune told. There isn't time today. I can hear our people returning to the dock. We'll have to say good-by. A thousand thanks."

Before Jenny knew it, she was flying through the streets with Jack Tar and her brothers. Soon she could hear what Jack's quick ears had detected minutes ago: the footsteps of passengers and sailors moving toward the dock.

"More speed!" cried Jack. "We're terribly late."

Jenny worked her little legs as fast as possible, and managed to keep up with the others. Presently she could see the lighter, still at the dock.

She and her brothers followed Jack Tar up the gangplank—just in time.

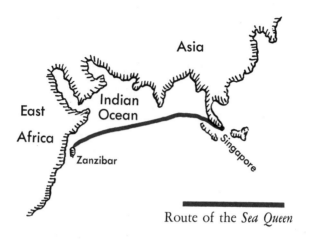

Route of the *Sea Queen*

On Their Way to the East

The lighter carried the cats to the *Sea Queen*, and they climbed aboard her safely. Jack Tar went to the bridge to help the Skipper * get the *Sea Queen* started on her way. Zanzibar gradually faded from sight. But the perfume of the island remained

* A skipper is the captain of a ship.

with the ship, for the Master of Freight had taken on a load of fragrant cloves.

And the memory of what had happened in Zanzibar haunted the young travelers. They were troubled by what the fortune-teller had predicted. So they separated, each to find a quiet spot to think things over.

Jenny curled up in an armchair in the empty lounge.

"It can't be true," she told herself. "I couldn't do something brave any more than Checkers could do something naughty. Maybe the fortuneteller made a mistake. But she read Edward's paw so well. I know he'll write a wonderful poem."

After a while, Jenny felt like talking with Edward. She found him lying under one of the lifeboats, murmuring:

> "In the old bazaar
> Of Zanzibar
> I heard my fortune told."

"Oh, Edward! How lovely!" Jenny exclaimed. "Is that the beginning of the great poem the fortuneteller said you'd write?"

Edward shook his head.

"No, it's just a little rhyme," he answered. "I haven't any idea what my big poem will be about. I won't know until the time comes."

Brother and sister remained silent for a moment.

Then Jenny said, "I'm worried about Checkers. I can't imagine him ever doing anything wicked."

"The fortuneteller didn't say wicked," Edward observed. "She said naughty, which isn't so bad. But anyway, we'll have to keep an eye on Checkers."

"And love him very hard," said Jenny. "Let's go find him."

They discovered their brother high in some ropes of the ship. He looked down with his same old adorable face. But when

he spoke he gave a queer, wild laugh they had never heard before.

"I have a naughty paw!" he cried excitedly.

"Nonsense," said Jenny. "You have a very good paw."

"I may get into trouble in the East," protested Checkers. "The fortuneteller said so."

"The fortuneteller was teasing you," Edward remarked calmly.

Checkers drew a sigh of relief, as if he'd rather be good than bad.

Just then Jack Tar joined the group. He seemed to guess what they had been discussing.

"If I were you," he said, "I'd forget Zanzibar, and do as the Skipper does and I myself and all the other sailors on this ship. Keep your minds on the next port of call and do your best to help the *Sea Queen* reach it."

"That's good advice," Edward declared. "And by the way, where are we bound?"

"We're bound for the East," Jack answered. "Our next port of call is Singapore."

Edward asked hopefully:

> "And go ashore
> In Singapore?"

"Why yes, I'll take you with me if you wish," said Jack. "All three of you did very well in the last port of call. Now remember, keep your minds on Singapore, and pray that we get there safely."

During the following days, the monsoon blew, but never too hard. And late one afternoon, just as the setting sun was coloring the waters with a thousand hues, the *Sea Queen* nosed up to her dock in Singapore.

All Ashore in Singapore

Jenny was wearing her red scarf when she joined her brothers and Jack at the head of the gangplank. Jack nodded with approval at the scarf.

"Days may be warm in Singapore," he remarked, "but nights are cool."

"A night in Singapore!" cried Checkers joyfully.

"No special plans, of course," said Jack. "We'll take things as they come. Let's go."

Jenny and her brothers followed the ship's cat down to the dock.

"First we'll stroll along the waterfront," said Jack. "It's fun to watch the ships in Singapore. They come from all over the world. Singapore is the busiest port in the East."

"Just what do you mean by the 'East'?" asked Checkers.

"The countries of Asia," replied Jack. "Lands like Malaya, where we are right now—and like Siam."

"Siam," murmured Checkers, with the little sigh of longing he always gave when he heard the land of his ancestors mentioned.

"Look!" continued Jack. "Out there in the harbor is a Chinese junk. I bet none of you has ever seen a junk."

The travelers gazed at the curious ship, whose yellow sail had ribs that looked like the veins in a leaf.

Suddenly Jack pointed to another pier on the waterfront.

"There's Bobo the Burmese," he exclaimed. "He's the young ship's cat on the freighter *Pride of the East*. But where is the *Pride*?"

The four cats hurried over to Bobo, who sat on the edge of the dock, staring in the direction of the open sea. When he heard the sound of their paws, he turned and cried out, "Jack! Jack Tar! How wonderful to meet you here."

"What happened?" asked Jack.

"I missed my ship," Bobo answered. And from the mournful tone of his voice, one could tell what a terrible thing it is when a sea cat misses his ship.

"How did it happen?" Jack asked with sympathy. "You may speak freely. These are friends of mine: Jenny, Checkers and Edward. They're passengers aboard the *Sea Queen*."

71

Bobo was a handsome young fellow with the rich, chocolate-colored fur that distinguishes the Burmese family of cats. To the end of her days Jenny would never forget his face as he told his tale of the sea.

"We were voyaging among the sunny islands of the Pacific Ocean," he began. "On the island of Hawaii I took shore leave. The kind Hawaiian people fed me fish and rice. I ate too much and fell asleep. When I woke up, I found myself beneath a palm tree with a wreath of flow-

ers around my neck. My ship, the *Pride of the East*, had sailed without me!"

"Oh dear," gasped Jenny. "What did you do?"

Bobo's face brightened as he replied, "I knew the route my ship would follow: the Philippines and then Siam and Singapore. I used my wits.

"I shipped aboard the next boat to the Philippines. She was a freighter, none too fast, and the *Pride* had pulled out of the Philippines a few days before we got there.

"But in the Philippines I had some luck. I caught a fast mail boat, the *Royal Rose*, and reached Siam only a few hours after the *Pride* had left. Then in the Gulf of Siam the *Royal Rose* outstripped the *Pride*, and we reached Singapore before she did. The *Pride* is due in Singapore tomorrow."

"Bobo," said Jenny, "I think it's wonderful the way you sea cats find your way around the world."

"Thank you," said Bobo. "But it's a disgrace to miss one's ship."

The mournful look returned to his face, and he lapsed into silence.

Finally Jack Tar broke the silence.

"Bobo," he said, "it's almost suppertime. We ought to get a bite to eat."

"A workman on the dock is feeding me right here," said Bobo. "I wouldn't want the *Pride* to come and go without me this time. But you four mustn't stay on my account."

"We won't go far," Jack promised. "I know a little restaurant near the dock. We'll get a snack and come right back."

Jack led his party to the restaurant, where they ordered a good Chinese meal of shrimp and rice. The cook seemed to understand why they ate quickly. For after they had finished and thanked him, he murmured something in a foreign language. But they caught the words *Bobo . . . Bobo . . . Bobo.*

The four cats found Bobo right where they had left him. They sat beside him quietly and watched the sun drop in the west. After a while night came. Stars twinkled gaily overhead, and moonshine covered the dock.

Jenny thought to herself, "It's a shame to waste the moonshine."

"Bobo," she said shyly, "everything will be all right. You'll catch your ship tomorrow. Tonight, why don't we have some fun?"

"How?" asked Bobo, and his voice still sounded mournful.

75

"We might dance," Jenny suggested. "It would be fun to dance along the waterfront."

"And so it would," Bobo agreed. "But I don't know the dances of the land cats."

"I can dance the sailor's hornpipe," Jenny said. "My master, Captain Tinker, showed me how."

"And Jenny taught me," Checkers said.

"And me," said Edward.

Then Bobo cried out merrily, "There's not a ship's cat on the Seven Seas who doesn't love to dance the hornpipe."

He stood up quickly on his two hind legs and held out a chocolate-colored paw to Jenny. She accepted it, and rose. And with her red scarf flying, she and the Burmese sea cat danced the hornpipe along the waterfront of Singapore.

Jack Tar danced behind them, with Checkers and Edward in tow. After a while the five cats changed partners. And after that they changed again. Finally they all danced together, paw to paw, until the moonshine vanished and the dawn arrived.

Early in the morning Bobo's ship, the *Pride of the East*, entered the harbor and docked where the cats were waiting. Bobo, of course, could hardly wait to climb aboard. But he lingered to thank once more the friends who had kept him company throughout the night.

To little Jenny he gave special thanks for making it a happy time.

"I hope we meet again," he told her.

Then he joined his ship to report for duty.

Jenny and her brothers and Jack Tar moved toward their own ship. They sailed at noon, bound for the port of Bangkok, in Siam—the land which Checkers longed to see.

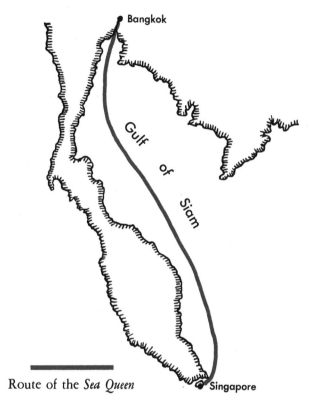

Route of the *Sea Queen*

Storm in the Gulf of Siam

They were crossing the Gulf of Siam
on their way to the land of Siam when the
monsoon blew up with the strength of a

thousand winds. The waves rose with an angry snarl and the *Sea Queen* tossed in a storm.

This was the first big storm that Jenny and her brothers had experienced. Jenny felt so frightened that her black fur stood on end.

"It isn't safe for you to stay on deck," Jack told her. "You and Checkers and Edward must go down to your cabin."

"Jack, where will you go?" Jenny asked.

"I've work to do on deck," he replied.

"We could help you," Edward volunteered.

"No, all passengers must go below," Jack said firmly.

The three young cats obeyed.

As they entered their cabin, the *Sea Queen* rolled so far on one side that they could barely stand. Then the ship straightened herself and lurched to the other side. The cats huddled together in a corner of the cabin while all night long the *Sea*

Queen battled the storm. Their master, Captain Tinker, did his best to comfort them. But it was really the ship's cat who kept up their spirits.

Every so often Jack would appear at their cabin door, his white fur dripping with the foam of the sea. But the patch of gray on top of his head stood upright like a crown of glory.

"I've just come down from the bridge," he would say. "All is well."

Jenny, Checkers and Edward felt that all would continue to be well aboard the *Sea Queen* as long as Jack Tar made the rounds, bringing comfort to passengers and crew.

Early in the morning the wind died away and the sea grew calm.

At breakfast time the three cats went down to the kitchen. Jack, covered by a warm wool blanket, lay asleep in a basket. The cook stood beside him, murmuring, "Jackie, the crew is proud of you. Now all you need is a bit of sleep and then some breakfast."

Checkers walked softly to the basket and with his pink tongue lovingly kissed the cheek of the sailor cat who had done so much to bring the *Sea Queen* safely through the storm.

Checkers Slips Away

The *Sea Queen* sailed out of the Gulf and headed up the river which leads to Bangkok, the capital of Siam.

Checkers sat at the ship's rail with the other cats. He saw the same things they saw: yellow blossoms adrift on the river, green marshes bordering the river's edge, and in the marshes strange little houses standing on poles.

But Jenny could feel that this brother of hers had thoughts of his own—thoughts which she could not possibly share. She understood why.

Checkers was entering the land where one of his ancestors had lived.

She could hear Checkers saying to Jack, "I can't wait till we get to Bangkok. I want to see everything there is to see—especially the Palace where the Royal and Sacred Cats of Siam used to live."

"Bangkok is a very big city," Jack explained. "We'll only be there twenty-four hours, and we can't see all the sights. I'll let Dara decide where we shall go."

"Who is Dara?" asked Checkers.

"She's the cat who lives in the big hotel by the river," replied Jack. "Her name, Dara, is Siamese for 'star.' "

"Is Dara a Siamese cat?" queried Checkers.

"One hundred per cent Siamese," Jack answered. "And she's a princess by birth."

Checkers' long tail swished with excitement. In all his life he had never met a cat one hundred per cent Siamese.

Now the port of Bangkok lies four miles from the main part of the city, where the hotel is situated. After the *Sea Queen* docked in the port, the cats climbed aboard a bus and rode to the hotel with other tourists from the ship.

They found Dara sitting on the hotel terrace, gazing at the river which flowed close by. She turned when she heard Jack's voice.

"Jack Tar!" she exclaimed. "How nice of you to come."

Jack bowed.

As for Checkers, he gazed adoringly at the young Siamese princess who was certainly one of the loveliest creatures in the world. Her eyes were a pure, light blue. Her fur was cream-colored, except for her ears and the lower part of her face; these were dark, seal brown. What interested Checkers most was Dara's tail. It was long and snaky, like his own.

She smiled at him.

"We must be cousins," she observed.

"One of my ancestors—maybe my grandfather—came from Siam," said Checkers bashfully. "But I was born in the United States."

"Then you are my American cousin," said Dara with a tinkling laugh.

"My name is Checkers," he informed her. "I'm traveling around the world with Jenny, Edward and Jack."

Dara looked at Jenny and said, "What a pretty scarf! Can you tie it on all by yourself?"

"My master, Captain Tinker, ties it on for me," replied Jenny.

Then Edward spoke up: "Our master is Master of Freight on this trip of the *Sea Queen*. We took on some wool in Capetown, some spices in Zanzibar and . . ."

"I know, I know," laughed Dara. "And some rubber in Singapore, and from Siam you'll sail away with fragrant teakwood. Freighters like the *Sea Queen* do good work. But the boats I love most are the little sampans on my river."

Dara waved a delicate paw toward the river, which was covered with hundreds of small, canoe-shaped boats, known as sampans.

Afterward she turned to Jack and asked, "How long will you remain in Bangkok?"

"Until tomorrow evening," he replied.

"I hope you and your friends will stop at our hotel," Dara continued. "The nights are warm—you wouldn't need a room. You could sleep quite comfortably on a bench in the hotel garden."

"Thank you, Dara," said Jack. "We accept your kind invitation."

As it was suppertime, Dara led her guests into the kitchen, where they dined on excellent prawns and rice. After that, she said, "Now we'll go sightseeing."

"I should love to visit the Royal Palace," said Checkers. "Maybe my grandfather lived there when he was a kitten."

"Cousin, the Palace is too far away."

"Couldn't we take a bus?" he asked.

The Siamese shook her head.

"To tell the truth," she explained, "I don't wish to go too near the Palace. I lived there until I ran away. If the Palace people found me, they might ask me to remain."

"Why did you run away?" asked Checkers.

"At the hotel I am free," replied Dara. "Whenever I please I may go down to the river and ride in my sampan. I'll take you with me tomorrow. Tonight it is proper for us to visit one of the temples for which Bangkok is famous."

The five cats walked along a street filled with noisy traffic. Then they entered a quiet enclosure and gazed at a temple where yellow-robed monks and other people came to worship. The walls of the temple were decorated with bits of brightly colored glass. The horn-shaped roof was covered with gold, and from the eaves hung rows of bells which tinkled in the wind.

"There are hundreds of these temples in Bangkok," whispered Dara. "That's why it's called the City of the Gods."

The cats were in a quiet mood as they returned to their hotel. Dara said goodnight and went to her room. Checkers, Jenny, Edward and Jack slept on a garden bench under the starry sky.

At the crack of dawn Dara roused them, crying, "Wake up, sleepyheads! Dawn is the best time in Bangkok."

The cats could feel the city stirring to life.

"I'll take you in my sampan to the Floating Market," continued Dara. "We'll eat breakfast out there on the river."

The five cats raced to the river's edge and entered a sampan. In the back of the sampan sat a little old woman who pushed an oar and moved the boat toward the Floating Market.

Checkers looked at Dara and said with a sigh, "I'd rather visit the Palace than eat."

"Cousin, I know what we'll do. After breakfast I'll take you up the river in my

91

sampan," she promised him. "From the
sampan you'll get a good view of the Palace,
which stands near the river."

"Couldn't we go ashore and really see
things?" he begged.

"No, cousin, no."

By this time the sampan was well out upon the river, threading its way among hundreds of other small boats. Sometimes in the distance a water bus hurried by. For here in Bangkok many of the streets are waterways instead of roads, and the people spend much of their time on the river, which is called Me Nam Chao Bhraya, meaning Royal Mother of Waters.

Now in the dawn the farmers were coming downstream to sell their vegetables at the Floating Market. Fishermen were bringing their fish. And a sampan went by, tinkling its bells.

"That's the ice-cream sampan," Dara explained. "But for breakfast it's wise to eat fish."

She waved to the woman at the oar, and they drew close to another sampan where fish was being sold. Here the boats were so close together you could almost touch them with your paw. Dara leaned forward and pointed to the fish. Jenny, Edward and Jack pointed, too, and the fisherman tossed some tasty bits into their sampan. The four cats devoured them hungrily.

"Delicious, wasn't it?" Edward remarked when they had finished.

He turned to Jenny and said, "You enjoyed yours, didn't you?"

"Oh, ever so much," she replied.

"And you, Checkers . . ." continued Edward.

Edward did not finish his sentence. For when he looked at the place where his brother had been, no one was there.

Jenny's heart almost stopped beating.

Jack said, "Checkers couldn't have fallen overboard. We would have heard him splash. Besides, the boats here are so thick there'd hardly be room for him in the river."

Dara laughed.

"My American cousin works fast indeed," she declared. "Look! He's jumped from boat to boat and taken the water bus to the Royal Palace."

Jenny, Edward and Jack stared up the river. In the back of a water bus they could see a black and white cat speeding toward the Royal Palace where maybe his grandfather lived in olden times.

Jenny Holds the Ship

"This is no joke," declared Jack. "Checkers has gone off on a lark. Now I'm afraid he'll have to pay for it."

"Pay for it!" exclaimed Jenny. "What do you mean?"

"I mean we'll have to let Checkers go," Jack replied sadly. "We haven't time to look for him. I'd miss my ship. Maybe on my next trip to Siam I can hunt for him, though there's the chance I'd never find him."

Then Edward said, "I shall go and find my brother. This is all my fault. I should have kept an eye on him. The fortuneteller warned us he'd get into trouble in the East."

"Edward, I wish I could go with you," said Jack. "It might take two of us to bring back Checkers. If only I didn't have to report to my ship."

Suddenly Jenny cried, "I have it."

"Have what?" asked Jack.

"A plan," she answered. "You and Edward will hunt for Checkers. I'll hold the ship until you come."

"Hold the ship!" exclaimed Jack. "How in the world could you keep the *Sea Queen* from sailing?"

"I'll stand in the middle of the gang-plank, so the sailors can't pull it up."

"What will you do if the sailors come and try to carry you on deck?" asked Jack.

"I'll scratch and bite if they come near me."

97

"What if they finally decide to pull the gangplank in?" asked Jack.

"Why then—why then—I'll drop into the river," she replied. "But I'll have done my best."

Jenny's black fur stood on end at the thought of what might happen "if." Yet just as calmly as she could she said, "The fortuneteller predicted I'd do something brave. Don't you remember?"

"And this may be it," agreed Jack. "There's no time to lose. Edward, let's start."

Dara, who had been listening to the plans, said, "I can help, too."

The Siamese was no longer a lighthearted princess playing gaily in her sampan on the river. Her long tail swished, and at a motion of her paw the sampan swung out to the route of the water buses. And there, since she was a Royal and Sacred Cat of Siam, one of the buses stopped to let Jack and Edward climb aboard for their journey to the Palace.

Dara and Jenny returned to the hotel. All day long they waited for the road bus that would carry Jenny to the *Sea Queen*. As they walked restlessly back and forth in the garden, they scarcely spoke. Their thoughts were elsewhere: sometimes on what might be happening at the Palace; sometimes on Jenny's dangerous plan to hold the ship.

At five o'clock in the afternoon the road bus arrived. In it were passengers and sailors from the *Sea Queen*, who had been seeing the sights in Bangkok.

Dara helped Jenny climb aboard.

"Good luck, Jenny," whispered the Siamese. "I know you can do it."

Then the bus sped toward the ship.

Sometimes the bus people talked to Jenny.

"Where is Jack Tar?" they would ask. "Where's Edward? Where's Checkers?"

But since Jenny was only a cat, she could not reply. Even if she had been able to speak human language, who would have believed the strange things that had happened in Bangkok?

When the bus reached the dock, the people climbed up the gangplank to the ship, while Jenny hid behind some barrels, biding her time.

Presently the flag, called the Blue Peter, was hoisted on the ship. This is the flag which means *ready to sail*.

"Now's the time," thought Jenny.

Bravely she climbed to the middle of the gangplank and then stood absolutely still.

A passenger caught sight of her and called out, "Come, Jenny, come."

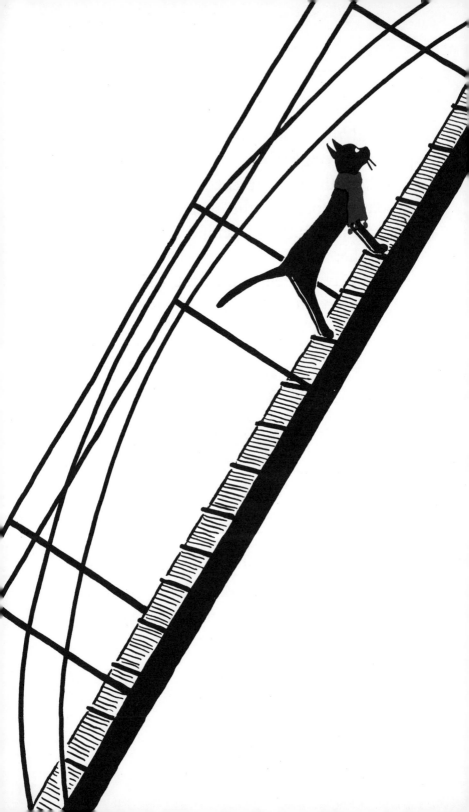

Jenny did not stir.

"Jenny, what's the matter?" cried a sailor.

"Come, Jenny, come." This time it was her master's voice.

Never had she disobeyed her master. But now she did not move a paw. Nor did she dare lift up her head and look at him to try to make him understand. It took all her strength to stand there on the scary gangplank. What if the sailors drew the gangplank in and dropped her into the river?

The minutes passed. They seemed like hours. Jenny's little legs could scarcely hold her any longer.

Suddenly, in the distance, she heard the rattlety-bang of a Bangkok road bus, racing toward the ship. Before she knew it, the bus stopped at the dock. The door flew open. Three cats jumped out and rushed to the foot of the gangplank.

Jenny could hear Jack say, "Steady, Checkers, steady. Keep your chin up."

The three cats joined Jenny on the gangplank.

"Fall in line," commanded Jack.

He led the way. Jenny came next, while Checkers and Edward brought up the rear. In this—their old—formation they followed the ship's cat safely to the deck.

It was the Skipper himself who complimented Jenny as she hurried past his legs.

"Good work, Jenny," he said. "Not every cat is brave enough to stand on a gangplank and hold the ship until her friends arrive."

Hammocks for All

Jack went to the bridge and helped the Skipper get the *Sea Queen* out of Bangkok.

Jenny and her brothers returned to their cabin. They felt badly shaken by the whole adventure, and their master stayed with them a while to comfort them. Not until he left them did they talk among themselves.

Then Checkers said, "I wonder if Jack will ever forgive me. I almost made him miss his ship."

"What happened?" Jenny asked gently.

"A spell came over me. A Siamese spell," he replied. "I felt all Siamese, and something mysterious pulled me to the Royal Palace."

"The fortuneteller warned us of trouble in the East," observed Edward.

"Yes," said Checkers. "Jenny has done her brave deed, and I have done my naughty deed."

He shook his right front paw.

"Now my wickedness has gone," he declared.

"And it's up to me to write a poem," said Edward. "Then all that the fortuneteller predicted will have come true."

They tried to laugh. But no one felt like being gay. Their thoughts were in Bangkok.

"What was the Palace like?" asked Jenny.

"All bright and glittering," Checkers replied. "And on the Palace grounds were temples with those tinkling bells. I met a Palace cat—a Siamese. He was showing me the stables for the white elephants when Edward and Jack Tar came running up. Jack was very angry, but I didn't want to leave. Then Edward told me you were standing on the gangplank. The spell upon me broke."

"Who was the bus driver who brought you to the ship?" asked Jenny.

"A friend of Jack's," said Checkers.

Jenny said, "I never knew a cat who had so many friends. Friends all over the world —in every port."

"I hope I'm still his friend," Checkers said nervously.

At suppertime the three travelers went into the kitchen, and Jack came down from the bridge.

"Jack! Jack Tar! Will you ever forgive me?" cried Checkers.

Jack had never looked so thoughtful as he did when he slowly gave his decision: "Checkers, you delayed the sailing of the *Sea Queen*, and that is a serious thing. But the Skipper seems to feel that what happened in Siam lay beyond our control. I agree with the Skipper."

Siam was not mentioned again. But the cats would never forget the dangerous experience they had shared. Somehow it brought them closer than before—so close that they spent all their waking hours with one another. Only at bedtime did they separate. Then Jack would go to his hammock on deck, while the young passengers returned to their cabin.

One evening as Jenny and her brothers were climbing the stairs on their way to bed they heard the ship's loud-speaker announcing, *Now hear you this. Jenny. Checkers. Edward. Report to Jack Tar.*

They rushed to the hammock deck, where they had just said good-night to Jack. They found him lying in his hammock, and next to it—lo and behold!—hung three other little hammocks.

"Not for us!" gasped Jenny.

"Yes," Jack replied with a grin. "The ship's carpenter rigged them up for you. He seems to think the four of us belong together."

Edward Writes a Poem

One night Jack Tar jumped from his hammock to make the rounds of the ship. As usual he looked to see that Jenny, Checkers and Edward were safe in their own hammocks. There they were, apparently asleep. But when Jack returned from his rounds, Edward had disappeared.

"Jenny! Checkers! Wake up!" cried Jack. They woke with a start.

"Where's Edward?" asked Jack. "He's not in his hammock."

"He was there when I went to sleep," said Jenny. "I could hear him whispering words to himself. Maybe he's gone off to write a poem."

"Can't he write in his hammock, like any other cat?" Jack asked impatiently.

"Not Edward," Jenny explained. "Writing is hard for him. He has to tie his tail in knots before a poem comes out of his head. And he has to be alone—all alone."

Then Checkers said, "Maybe he's busy with that poem the fortuneteller in Zanzibar predicted."

"Well," said Jack, "I only hope he hasn't fallen overboard."

Jenny and Checkers gasped at the thought. They jumped from their hammocks and followed Jack as he climbed to the bridge and began to search the ship from top to bottom.

Half an hour later they found Edward in the farthest corner of the engine room. In his eyes lurked a dreamy, satisfied look.

"Did you write a poem?" asked Jenny.

"Yes," he replied, "it's an ode—a poem in praise of."

"In praise of what?" asked Jack, whose knowledge of poetry was limited to old sea chanties.

"In praise of a ship's cat," Edward replied.

Jack pricked up his ears. "That could be interesting—at least for those of us who follow the sea. How does it go?"

Edward shyly began to mumble some lines. But Jenny said, "Not in the engine room, with all these noises. We can't hear you properly. Come on deck."

They returned to the hammock deck and there Edward recited his poem:

> "How shall we get there?
> When will it be?
> Trust in the ship's cat,
> All of ye.
>
> Lolling in his hammock
> Instead of a bed,
> Bounding on the high seas,
> Full steam ahead—
>
> Jack Tar, the ship's cat,
> Guides the good *Sea Queen*
> Underneath the starry skies
> To her port unseen."

"What a beautiful poem," exclaimed Jenny, when Edward had finished. "Don't you think so, Jack?"

"Shiver my whiskers," Jack said happily. "I wish the Skipper could have heard it."

Then Checkers said, "Now all that the fortuneteller in Zanzibar predicted has come true. I got into trouble; Jenny did a brave deed; Edward has written his poem."

"And the voyage is far from over," Jack Tar observed. "We're only on the China Sea."

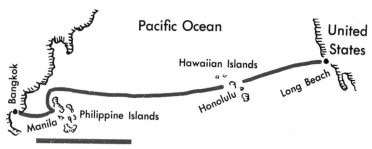

Route of the *Sea Queen*

After they left the China Sea they sailed across the blue Pacific. Warm, sunny days slipped into nights and the nights into the days so quietly that you could scarcely tell where time had gone.

Among the islands of the Pacific the ship touched at Manila, where the cats ate excellent fish and rice, and the Master of Freight took on a load of coconuts.

Next they visited Honolulu, where the Master of Freight took on some pineapples, and the four cats ate a different kind of fish and rice and returned to the ship wearing those little wreaths of flowers, called leis, which the kind Hawaiian people hang around the necks of visitors.

From Honolulu they made the long, unbroken trek across the remainder of the Pacific until they reached the port of Long Beach, California, on the west coast of the United States. In Long Beach they went into a drugstore, sat at a counter and ordered hamburger without the bun.

"There's nothing like a good old hamburger," Edward observed. "Especially after all that fish we ate in the East."

Coconut

Pineapple

Blue Peter

Sunny days

Hawaiian leis

Ordering

Fish and rice

Hamburger without bun

Sketches from
Captain Tinker's diary

"This is almost like being home," said Checkers.

But to little Jenny, Long Beach didn't seem at all like home, even though it was in the United States. Home to her meant New York and the Cat Club and Pickles the fire cat who protected the Club from fires.

To reach New York, which lay on the east coast of the United States, they had to sail south to a narrow neck of land called Panama. Here a great ditch, the Panama Canal, had been dug so that ships might cross from the Pacific to the Atlantic Ocean.

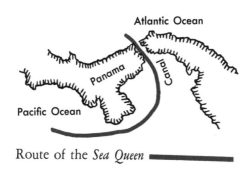

Route of the *Sea Queen* ■━━━━

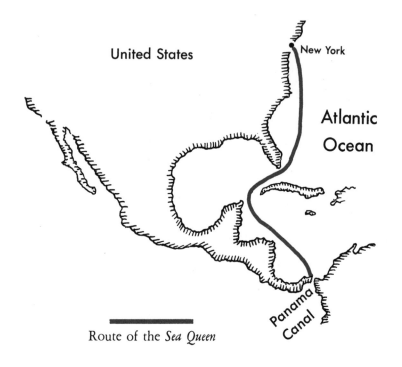

United States

New York

Atlantic
Ocean

Route of the *Sea Queen*

Panama
Canal

Home from the Sea

The four cats were sitting on deck when the *Sea Queen* left the Panama Canal and entered broader waters.

"We're back on the Atlantic," explained Jack. "New York lies just a few days north. You'll soon be home."

"Home!" exclaimed Checkers. "I wish this voyage would never have to end."

"We've made such friends at sea," said Edward, looking straight at Jack.

Suddenly Jenny thought to herself, "After we reach New York Jack Tar will sail away. Wouldn't it be terrible if we didn't see him again."

"Jack," she said slowly, "did you ever think of giving up the sea and living on the land?"

"I'll sail as long as I can serve the *Sea Queen*," replied Jack.

"And after that?" asked Jenny.

"Most sea cats have a dream," Jack answered. "It's this: that when we grow too old to sail we'll settle on the land. Maybe with a little luck I'll find a home in someone's house—perhaps a pink brick house

119

that has a rosebush in the garden."

"Why, that's the kind of house our master has!" cried Jenny. "I'm sure he'd like to have you come and live with us."

"But that's a long time off—too long to think about," insisted Jack. "There's many a year of work ahead of me."

Jenny thought a moment. Then she asked him, "What will you do when the *Sea Queen* reaches New York?"

"They'll have to paint the ship and get her ready for another voyage around the world," said Jack. "That takes about a week or so. I'll get shore leave, of course, and knock about the docks."

"Knock about the docks!" exclaimed Jenny. "Jack Tar, you're going to spend shore leave with us."

"Indeed you are," Edward said firmly. "Now we must arrange to get you there."

It was Checkers who thought up the plan.

"Jack," he said, "when the *Sea Queen* reaches New York, Captain Tinker will get out our traveling baskets. Edward and I will squeeze into my basket, and you'll get into Edward's. Then Captain Tinker will understand you're to come with us."

"Your master will have an extra mouth to feed," Jack said thoughtfully.

"But he won't mind," Jenny cried warmly. "Not after all you've done for us. And I'm sure he'll bring you back to your ship when she's ready to sail."

"And if he didn't—if he couldn't," said Jack, "I'd get there on my own four paws. A ship's cat always manages."

Their last night at sea—their last few hours aboard the ship—arrived at last.

At midnight Jack got down from his hammock.

"I'll make my rounds as usual," he said. "Afterward I'll join the Skipper on the bridge and help him bring the *Sea Queen* into New York Harbor."

Jenny, Checkers and Edward jumped from their hammocks, too, and strolled on deck. Sometimes they paused and gazed out across an ocean all dappled with moonlight. Sometimes they stood in the prow and listened to the *Sea Queen* slicing through the waters on the last lap of her voyage.

Dawn came. The sky grew rosy and finally clear blue.

On the right they saw a little freighter sailing out to sea. On the left, a huge, fast vessel heading homeward, like themselves.

Suddenly Jack called down from the bridge, "Land ahead!"

It looked like a blur at first. But as the ship drew nearer and nearer the buildings took shape and resembled fairy castles rising from the sea to touch the sky.

"Of all the wonders of the world, we've seen nothing more beautiful than this," said Edward.

"Isn't it lucky I didn't get stuck in Siam," murmured Checkers.

But the little black cat, Jenny Linsky, said nothing.

She stared straight ahead, her eyes fixed on the city, which seemed to grow bigger and bigger, with thousands of buildings and millions and millions of windows.

Jenny could hardly believe that somewhere in all that bigness there could be a home for her.

Besides, she had been gone so long. Around the world! What if the Cat Club had forgotten her? What if her old friend, Pickles, hadn't remembered?

All at once she heard a siren wailing near the *Sea Queen*. It sounded like the siren on Pickles' fire truck.

Jenny glanced down at the harbor and saw coming toward the *Sea Queen* a small boat rigged out with fire hose. In the prow sat a spotted cat whose helmet had been polished till it shone like new.

"Pickles!" she cried. "Oh, Pickles!"

"Hi, Jenny!" called the fire cat. "Hi, Checkers! Hi, there, Edward!"

"Pickles," asked Checkers, "how did you know we were coming today?"

"The Cat Club kept in touch with the waterfront," replied Pickles. "The long-shore cat told us the *Sea Queen* was due this morning. And the Fire Department let me get on board this fire boat."

Then Jenny asked, "How's everyone at home?"

"Fine. Just fine," said Pickles. "All the Club is waiting for you in Captain Tinker's garden. They'll give a party for you as soon as you arrive."

Then he added happily, "It's like old times to have you back."

At that moment Jack came down from the bridge.

"Pickles," said Jenny, "this is Jack Tar, the ship's cat. He's going to spend shore leave with us."

Pickles' shoulders sagged.

Jenny felt that for some strange reason Pickles might be jealous of Jack.

"But that's not like Pickles," she reasoned with herself. "He's always generous. I guess he doesn't understand the noble work Jack does at sea."

"Pickles!" she cried. "Jack Tar is the ship's cat. Don't you understand? He helps run the *Sea Queen*, just as you help run the New York City Fire Department."

Pickles understood.

His shoulders straightened, and his right paw touched his helmet in salute.

"Welcome," he cried gaily. "Welcome to Jack Tar."

And Jenny felt she was home at last— home from the sea.

ESTHER AVERILL (1902–1992) began her career as a storyteller drawing cartoons for her local newspaper. After graduating from Vassar College in 1923, she moved first to New York City and then to Paris, where she founded her own publishing company. The Domino Press introduced American readers to artists from all over the world, including Feodor Rojankovsky, who later won a Caldecott Award.

In 1941, Averill returned to the United States and found a job in the New York Public Library while continuing her work as a publisher. She wrote her first book about the red-scarfed, mild-mannered cat Jenny Linsky in 1944, modeling its heroine on her own shy cat. Averill would eventually write twelve more tales about Miss Linsky and her friends (including the I Can Read Book *The Fire Cat*), each of which was eagerly awaited by children all over the United States (and their parents, too).

.

TITLES IN THE NEW YORK REVIEW
CHILDREN'S COLLECTION

ESTHER AVERILL
Jenny and the Cat Club

ESTHER AVERILL
Jenny Goes to Sea

ESTHER AVERILL
Jenny's Birthday Book

DINO BUZZATI
The Bears' Famous Invasion of Sicily

EILÍS DILLON
The Island of Horses

ELEANOR FARJEON
The Little Bookroom

RUMER GODDEN
An Episode of Sparrows

NORMAN LINDSAY
The Magic Pudding

ERIC LINKLATER
The Wind on the Moon

BARBARA SLEIGH
Carbonel: The King of the Cats

T. H. WHITE
Mistress Masham's Repose

REINER ZIMNIK
The Crane